Autumn
Publishing

Published in 2019
by Igloo Books Ltd
Cottage Farm
Sywell
NN6 0BJ
www.igloobooks.com

LEO002 0319
2 4 6 8 10 9 7 5 3 1
ISBN 978-1-78905-249-7

Printed and manufactured in China

THIS BOOK
BELONGS TO:

In Andy's bedroom, Sheriff Woody was in charge of all the toys and he loved his life with his friends. He was very careful to look after everyone, so when he realised that RC had been left outside one night, he leapt into action with his good friend Bo Peep.

"Operation Pull-Toy!" they shouted together.

Woody held onto Slinky Dog
and jumped out of the window.
Bo used her hook to lower Slinky
even further so Woody could reach
RC and pull him out of the mud.

When RC was free, all the toys,
apart from Woody, made it to
safety just as a stranger's car
pulled into the driveway.

All alone in the garden, Woody cautiously peered through the window.
He was shocked to see Andy's mum carefully placing Bo and her sheep
in a box – Bo was being given away to a different kid! Woody quickly
launched a new rescue mission – he had to get to Bo!

While the stranger was busy looking for his car keys, Woody opened the box but Bo didn't move.

"It's time for the next kid," said Bo, gently. For a moment, Woody considered climbing in the box with her, but he knew he couldn't leave Andy. Bo straightened Woody's hat one last time, wiped a raindrop from his face and settled down in the box with her sheep. Then, she was gone.

Years later, and after many adventures together, Andy gave his toys to a little girl called Bonnie. The toys settled in to their new home but, as time went on, Woody found he was played with less and less.

One day, Bonnie went to her settling in session at preschool. To make sure she was okay, Woody sneaked into her backpack and secretly went with her.

At preschool, Bonnie felt very unsure and tearful but she soon started to enjoy herself when, with a little bit of secret help from Woody, she made a pencil holder called Forky. She immediately loved him and carefully put him in her bag to take him home. Woody got a huge shock when, in the darkness of Bonnie's bag, he saw one of Forky's googly eyes move. He was alive!

The other toys were pleased when Woody safely returned to the bedroom but they were very surprised that he had come back with a talking spork!

"Everyone," said Woody. "I want you to meet Forky." Woody quickly explained to the startled toys that Forky was important to Bonnie and that he would help her settle in at preschool.

"We all have to make sure nothing happens to him," he said.

Poor Woody soon discovered that looking after Forky wasn't that easy. The spork believed he was a piece of rubbish and kept jumping in the bin!

With a few days to spare before Bonnie started preschool full-time, the family decided to have a holiday in their campervan. The journey wasn't easy for Woody because every time the family stopped for snacks or fuel, Forky ran to the nearest rubbish bin! Luckily, Woody was always there to stop him.

Later that night, Bonnie's dad carried on driving while his family slept in the campervan.

Suddenly, the toys realised that Forky was missing and spotted him standing at an open window!

"I am not a toy," he declared. "I'm a spork." And with that, Forky jumped out of the moving campervan before the toys could stop him.

Woody climbed up to the window and jumped down to the bumper. Then, the van hit a pothole and Woody tumbled out of the campervan to the road below!

Woody called to his friends that he would meet them at the RV park and ran off after Forky.

TriCounty RV
CALL TO RENT!

On the road, Forky was enjoying his freedom but Woody soon caught up with him and dragged him in the direction of the RV park.

"Like it or not, you are a toy," said Woody.

Woody explained how important toys are to kids. Finally, Forky started to understand how much he meant to Bonnie.

"She must be feeling awful without me," said Forky, breaking into a run. "We got to get going, she needs me!"

When they reached the town of Grand Basin, Woody noticed an old lamp in the window of an antique shop. It looked very familiar.

"Bo..." said Woody.

Woody had to know if it really was Bo's lamp and crawled through the shop's letterbox with Forky. In the shop, Woody and Forky met a doll called Gabby Gabby and a ventriloquist's dummy called Benson.

She asked if they were lost.

"No, but we are looking for a lost toy," Woody replied. "Name's Bo Peep?"

"Yes! I know Bo," said Gabby Gabby. "We'll take you to her."

Then, Gabby Gabby noticed Woody's voice box and told him it would be a perfect replacement for her broken one. Woody started to feel nervous and tried to leave.

"You can't leave," Gabby Gabby said. "You have what I need."

Just as the shop owner and her granddaughter, Harmony, arrived to open up, Woody and Forky found themselves surrounded by a group of dummies. One of them grabbed Forky and, without any other options, Woody pulled his string. The noise made Harmony notice Woody and she decided to take him to the park. The dummies held Forky as they helplessly watched Harmony carry Woody out of the shop.

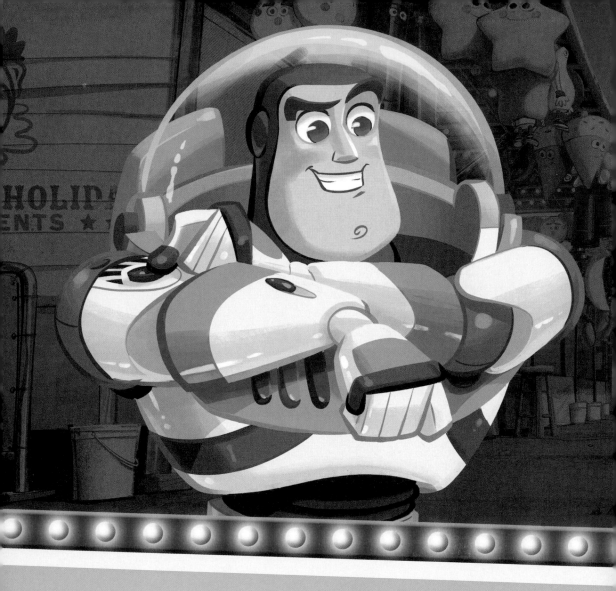

Back in the campervan, Bonnie tearfully searched everywhere for Forky. The toys had never seen their kid so upset and knew they had to do something. Buzz told the toys that he would go and find Woody and Forky, then he jumped out of the window!

The main road was the last place Buzz had seen Woody so he decided that was the best place to start looking for him. The quickest route led him through a carnival that had set up in the town.

Buzz zig-zagged his way through the rides until a carnival worker knocked him down! Seconds later, Buzz found himself strapped to the prize wall of one of the games.

"Step right up!" the carnival worker yelled into the crowd. "Get yourself a real Buzz Lightyear!"

Harmony was having great fun playing with Woody at the park. Although he enjoyed having some playtime, Woody was also busy plotting how he could get back to Forky. As soon as he got a chance, he sprinted through the packed and chaotic playground.

Suddenly, he was distracted by a very familiar sight. He turned and noticed a girl playing with a toy on the merry-go-round. As he tried to get a closer look, the girl picked Woody up and introduced him to her other toy – Bo Peep!

Bo and Woody were thrilled to see each other and, at the first opportunity, they headed to a hideaway. A vehicle disguised as a skunk skidded to a stop next to them.

"Hold on there!" laughed Woody as Bo's sheep jumped out of the skunkmobile and tackled him. "I missed you, too!"

Bo explained how she was stuck in the antique shop for years. Now, she was a lost toy and loved being free to go wherever she wanted.

Bo introduced Woody to her tiny friend Giggle McDimples. Woody asked them both to help him rescue Forky. Bo and Giggle were reluctant to go back to the antique shop where they had spent many unhappy years.

"Kids lose toys every day," shrugged Bo. "Bonnie will get over it." Woody reminded Bo about her first kid, Molly. She reluctantly agreed to help. Everyone piled into the skunkmobile and they zoomed away.

In the carnival game, Buzz was doing his best to escape but two of the other prize toys, Ducky and Bunny, started shouting at him. They weren't happy that Buzz had taken their place as the top prize!

"If you think you can just show up and take our top prize spot, you're wrong!" shouted Bunny.

"C'mon," replied Buzz. "Help me outta here."

"I'll help you," Ducky said. "With my foot!"

Ducky started kicking at Buzz's head while Bunny swung him. Buzz didn't know what to do, so he shut his helmet. The helmet closed on Ducky's foot and he was able to pull himself out of the plastic tie that held him in place. The three toys struggled and fell to the ground in a heap!

Buzz was free and his mission to rescue Woody was back on!

On the way to the antique shop,
Bo told Woody all about her
new life.

"Who needs a kid's room when
you can have all of this?" she
asked, looking out at the carnival.

Meanwhile, just as he was
trying to work out what to do
next, Buzz looked up and saw
Woody jumping to the roof of the
antique shop. He climbed up to
meet him and was surprised to see
Bo! He was even more surprised
when Ducky and Bunny also
appeared. The squabbling toys
even agreed to help with the rescue
mission in return for a place in
Bonnie's room.

"You're gonna have to follow my lead," said Bo to all the toys as she leapt down the airshaft into the shop.

Still upset about losing Forky, Bonnie and her mum searched all over the campervan.

"Let's look outside one more time," said Bonnie's mum. "Then we have to keep driving, okay?"

Jessie was horrified to hear that the family planned to drive off without Buzz, Woody and Forky

"We have to stop them!" cried Jessie, as she told the other toys what was happening.

Jessie jumped out of the window and the toys suddenly heard a loud hissing sound.

"We're not going anywhere... if you get my point," said Jessie, re-appearing and showing the huge nail she had used to pop the van's tyre!

In the antique shop, Bo showed the toys where she thought Forky was being kept. It looked impossible to get to him – especially as a vicious cat called Dragon roamed the shop, but Bo had a plan.

All of a sudden, the door of the shop flew open and Woody heard a familiar voice. It was Bonnie!

"We gotta get Forky now!" gasped Woody as he ran towards the cabinet.

Suddenly, Benson grabbed Woody and one of Bo's sheep bit onto Benson's trousers.

In the confusion, the dummy ran off with the sheep still attached to him.

Now Gabby Gabby had Forky and Bo's sheep!

Bo took Woody to a secret hangout inside an old pinball machine. She knew just the person to help them jump across the aisle to Gabby Gabby's cabinet - Duke Caboom, Canada's greatest stuntman.

"Look who jumped forty school buses and landed back in my life," said Duke as he rode his motorcycle over to Bo.

Duke started showing off and stood in lots of different poses on his bike. When he had finally finished, Bo told him that they needed his help to rescue her sheep and Forky. All they needed him to do was jump across the aisle on his motorcycle.

"No!" exclaimed Duke. "Nuh-uh. Negative. Rejected!"

Woody tried to convince Duke to help by telling him all about Bonnie, but this triggered some very unhappy memories for the stuntman.

Duke sobbed as he remembered Rejean, his kid. Rejean was so excited to have his own Duke Caboom until he realised that he didn't jump like the one on the TV advert!

"Forget your commercial," said Bo. "Be the Duke you are right now. The one who jumps and crashes."

Bo's encouragement started to work and she once again asked Duke if he could do the jump.

"Yes I Canada!" said a newly enthusiastic Duke.

Giggle and the rest of the toys joined them and revealed they had managed to grab the key to the cabinet!

Finally, the mission was underway but it all went wrong very quickly when Duke lost his confidence again and crashed into Dragon.

Bo grabbed her sheep just as the cat chased all the toys through the shop, but Forky was still with the dummies.

Outside, Dragon ran off and the toys were shaken by their narrow escape.

They couldn't believe it when Woody insisted that they needed to go back and get Forky. He told them again that Bonnie needed Forky, but Bo saw things very differently.

"No, you need Bonnie," said Bo. "There's plenty of kids out there. It can't just be about the one you're still clinging to."

Bo started walking away, she planned to leave with the carnival in the morning. Even Buzz didn't want to go in the shop again and he headed back to the campervan. Woody was on his own.

Back in the shop, Woody found himself face-to-face with Gabby Gabby. Forky had told her everything about Woody's life and Gabby Gabby longed to be important to a kid like Woody was. Woody knew she was talking about Harmony. "I'd give anything to be loved the way you have," said Gabby Gabby.

"Just leave me Forky," said Woody, knowing what he had to do. "Bonnie needs him."

Gabby Gabby was delighted with her new voice box. It worked perfectly! Finally, she believed her dream was about to come true and Harmony would play with her and love her forever.

Woody and Forky were reunited just as Woody heard Bonnie and her mum enter the shop. They both headed for the backpack that Bonnie had accidentally left in the shop the day before.

Meanwhile, Gabby Gabby placed herself near Harmony as she pulled her own string.

"I'm Gabby Gabby, and I love you," she said.

Harmony picked up Gabby Gabby and her grandmother told her that she could keep the doll if she wanted her.

"Nah," Harmony replied. "Too creepy."

Then, Harmony chucked Gabby Gabby back in her pram.

Woody and Forky were shocked and Woody had to think fast. He told Forky to get Buzz to somehow bring the campervan to the carnival. Then, he jumped out of the bag just as Bonnie picked it up and left the shop.

Woody had a plan. He wanted to help Gabby Gabby and went over to where Harmony had dumped her.

"You can have your voice box back," Gabby Gabby told Woody, sadly. "I don't need it anymore."

He knew that Harmony wasn't her only chance to get a kid and told her that Bonnie would love to have her.

"You still have everything it takes to love a child – any child," said Woody.

As he kindly encouraged her, Bo overheard their conversation. She had returned with the other toys to help and was incredibly proud to hear what Woody told Gabby Gabby.

Bo and Giggle jumped down from the top of the pram where they had been listening to Woody. They wanted to help Woody get Gabby Gabby to Bonnie.

As they started to make their way through the park, Gabby Gabby noticed a girl crying and wanted to help her.

"Change of plans," said Woody.

The toys moved Gabby Gabby near the lost girl and pulled the doll's string. "Hi there. I'm Gabby Gabby. Will you be my friend?" she said.

The girl picked up the doll and hugged her tight. "Are you lost, too?" she asked. "It's okay, don't be scared."

The girl built up the courage to ask a security guard for help and she clung to Gabby Gabby as they searched for her parents. Gabby Gabby finally had a kid.

Thrilled that they had done a great thing for Gabby Gabby, Woody and Bo were reunited with the other toys. Everyone was happy to see them and Woody was even happier to see Bonnie reunited with Forky – he had successfully done the job that he had set out to do.

Woody loved seeing kids playing with toys and toys finding happiness with kids. Woody realised that helping kids and toys made him happy.

Woody's adventure with a spork who didn't want to be a toy and Bo, who had
proved that being a lost toy wasn't as terrible as Woody imagined, had taught
Woody how much he enjoyed helping kids and toys.

Woody didn't know what his next adventure would be but he did know that
wherever he went and whichever toy he helped next, anything would be possible
with great friends by his side.

THE END